I0518284

SUPERVILLAIN OF THE DAY

Short Stories:

SUPERVILLAIN
OF THE DAY

SUPERHERO
OF THE
DAY

KATIE LYNN
DANIELS

Cover design by Jasmine Ruigrok
Interior formatting by Aubrey Hansen

Special thanks to Elizabeth Kirkwood for proofreading, to BushMaid for the amazing cover design, to Joel Parisi for his endless typo-hunting, and to Aubrey for formatting and being my biggest fan. I couldn't have done it without you guys.

Published by:
Provide Your Own – Books
PO Box 748
Tompkinsville, KY 42167
Website: Books.ProvideYourOwn.com

Print Edition, April 2014
ISBN-13: 978-0615986807 (Provide Your Own - Books)
ISBN-10: 0615986803
Library of Congress Control Number: 2014904706

For Sian
For being the bravest person I know

TABLE OF CONTENTS

IT'S A RAT!
IT'S A PEST!
IT'S—

One giant metal foot came crashing down on the pavement, squashing an entire intersection. The second one landed right next to it, going clean through the roof of a petrol station. The owner of the two metal feet stood oblivious to the damage he had done; too bent on causing more. He rubbed one giant metal fist with the other, and his giant metal head swiveled from side to side, eagerly anticipating his next move.

Everyone ran screaming away from him, desperate to avoid being squashed by the next step. They were all as small as insects to the giant metal man, who remained planted in the intersection for an unreasonably long time until they were all gone. All but one.

"Puny mortal," said the giant metal man in a giant metal voice that reverberated through the clouds overhead, setting off an electrical storm a few miles away. "For what purpose do you remain in my path, knowing that I will destroy you with my next step?"

The puny mortal spoke into a puny microphone, and his voice boomed out over hidden speakers loudly enough to be heard over the electrical storm caused by the giant metal voice.

"I am the Defender of Earth," the puny mortal said. "You shall not pass."

The giant metal man laughed a giant metal laugh.

"You are but an ant beneath my shoe," he taunted. "A gnat within my fingers. I shall crush you the way a boy crushes a bug to impress a girl."

The Defender of Earth paused for a moment. "This conversation is getting a little weird," he commented.

The giant metal man paused also. "Is it?" he said. "I hadn't noticed."

"The bit about impressing a girl," the Defender of Earth clarified. "I thought that was a bit uncomfortable."

"Oh," said the giant metal man. "Sorry."

The Defender of Earth waved a hand in dismissal. "Think nothing of it."

"Uh... where were we?" asked the giant metal man.

"You were about to squash me," the Defender of Earth offered helpfully. "Like a bug."

"I shall squash you like a bug!" the giant metal man recapped. "Like an ant beneath my giant metal shoe."

He lifted one foot and brought it back down for emphasis. When the dust settled and the earthquake subsided the Defender of Earth could be clearly heard saying:

"You missed."

The giant metal man looked down at his foot as though seeing it for the first time.

"Oh," he said again. "So I did."

He was waiting for a response, so he didn't notice when the puny mortal dropped the microphone and moved. A moment later he felt something smack against the back of his giant metal head, but when he whacked at it with one giant metal hand it was already gone and he only succeeded in knocking himself off balance. And a moment after that a hatch in the back of the giant metal head was wrenched open and the Defender of Earth dropped into the control room within.

Four frightened henchmen in blue uniforms looked up from their instruments, and a supervillain dressed all in black stood up so quickly that he tripped on his long black cloak. The Defender of Earth grinned at them, and reeled in his grappling hook.

"The thing about bugs," said Jeffry Lewis Floyd, "is that they can be elusive little buggers."

"Get him!" roared the supervillain.

The control room descended into pandemonium and chaos.

❮ ❮ ❮

The great Supervillain Research Center on Alpha-Gamma-Gemini-seven-two-four had spent a very long time coming up with ways to combat the supervillain threat. Their methods ranged from implausible to absurd. Most were highly unethical, and all were wildly expensive. And yet they had come no closer to a solution than a ten-year-old school child who proposed throwing rocks and then running away very fast.

The great Superhuman Research and Development center in Phoenix, AZ, USA, Planet Earth had a slightly better plan. Create beings equally powerful as the supervillains, and somehow make sure they don't turn evil. They got this idea from inventors of fiction who write in a medium knows as "comic books." The rest of the galaxy didn't have comic books, which was just one of the many reasons they were so eager to open trade negotiations with Earth.

The Galactic Department of Supervillain Help and Relief Services decided that the best way to deal with the supervillain threat was to learn everything you could about them and target their weaknesses and generally cope as best as you could. This was a remarkably sensible idea until they amended it to "Force someone else to learn everything in existence about supervillains and target their weaknesses" on their behalf. This turned out to be a stupendously good idea because it only required one person to be inconvenienced instead of an entire race. The only one who hated the idea was the person forced to learn everything in existence about supervillains, which was actually quite a bit since the problem had been around for half a millennium. But since no one listened to him anyway it was universally decided to give this idea a go.

The four henchmen in blue leapt simultaneously towards the intruder, who counter-attacked by swinging his hook towards them, grappling them all into a jumble of squalling arms and legs. He tried to reel them in, but the hook had become caught on something else as well. Something sort of lever-shaped with a large label next to it that read "Equilibrium stabilizers."

Outside, the giant metal man was shaking his head from side to side as if something inside was bothering him. Then, very slowly, he began to fall.

Inside the giant metal head the henchmen, supervillain, and intruder all held onto each other and screamed as they descended rapidly onto the city below.

When the dust subsided and the earth stop quaking the Defender of Earth and the supervillain of the day pulled themselves out of the ruins and stared at each other.

The Defender of Earth moved first, shrugging and jumping forward with the remnants of his grappling hook in one hand. The supervillain tried to run, but the other was faster and soon had him firmly in hand, the thin black cord wrapped around his neck.

"Not such a bug now, am I?" Floyd whispered into the villain's ear.

The villain gasped and clawed at the cord, but there would be no escape for him.

"I'm—still—taller," he choked out.

Frowning, Floyd jerked the cord tighter. "Not by much," he countered. "Well, maybe a little. And who's winning in this scenario despite height differences?"

The supervillain tried to make a witty comeback, but he was rather short of breath.

Floyd laughed and was about to make another comment, but was interrupted by someone kicking him in the spine. He let go of the villain and fell forwards onto him. The villain chose this opportunity to roll away from his captor and unwind the cord from around his neck. Both glared up at the interloper.

Towering above them was a masked figure in a blue suit; floor length cape swirling behind him as he look down majestically with both hands balled into fists, waiting for either combatant to make a move. The villain opened his mouth and shut it without saying anything. Floyd stared.

"Are you seeing this?" the villain asked finally.

Floyd nodded.

"How hard did we fall?"

Floyd shrugged.

"Maybe he's not real," the villain suggested anxiously, scrambling to his feet. "Maybe if we just..."

His hand brushed against a knee encased in blue spandex, and the villain was instantly rewarded for his forward behavior by a swift punch to the jaw that knocked him out entirely. Floyd decided to take action.

"See here," he asked in annoyance. "Who are you and what are you doing interrupting disputes of a personal nature?"

"I am the Blue Shadow," the stranger said in an intimidating tone. "I am the swift sword of justice. I bring fear and confusion to my enemies."

"I see," Floyd said, unimpressed. "And who would be your enemies, exactly?"

"I fight against the supervillains," the Blue Shadow said proudly.

"Wearing that?" Floyd said dubiously, scrambling to his feet a safe distance away. "Calling yourself the Blue Shadow? What do you think you are; a superhero of some kind?"

With a dramatic gesture the Blue Shadow bowed. "At your service," he said.

"You're insane," Floyd said decisively. "You know what happens to superheroes in this town? They get killed. Do you know what happens to superheroes on this *planet*? They get killed. So why don't you go home and change into something a little less of an eye-sore before you *get killed*?"

The Blue Shadow laughed. Floyd caught a shade of condescension creeping into that laugh and it annoyed him.

"I'm serious," he said.

"I can take care of myself," the Blue Shadow assured him.

"No you can't," Floyd snorted. "No one can take care of themselves. Fighting supervillains is my job. Rescuing imbeciles—not so much."

"I'm quite sure I won't need any rescuing from you," the Blue Shadow assured him, looking down from his superior height. Behind him the supervillain slowly got to his feet.

"Riiight," Floyd said. "Because you have this situation so completely under control."

The supervillain glanced questioningly at Floyd. Floyd shrugged.

"Of course I do," the Blue Shadow retorted.

The supervillain made a rude gesture towards the hero's back.

"Uh huh," Floyd agreed, and grinned at the villain.

The Blue Shadow frowned. "What are you laughing at?"

Floyd pretended to be surprised. "Me? Nothing," he said. "Other than you, of course."

To the villain he mouthed the word "rematch."

"And you are...what, exactly?" the Blue Shadow asked.

The villain gave a thumbs up and sauntered away. Floyd grinned and turned his attention back to the interloper.

"Me?" he said, raising an eyebrow. "I'm nobody. Jeffry Lewis Floyd. Defender of the Earth. Supervillain Consultant for Scotland Yard. This is my business, and you're stepping in it."

The Blue Shadow seemed to perk up considerably. "You're with the police?" he said. "Even better. I wish to work in complete cooperation with local authorities."

"Well maybe we don't want to cooperate with you," Floyd retorted. "Have you thought of that?"

"Very cute," the Blue Shadow said dryly. "I'd like to talk to your superior officer, please."

"I don't have one," Floyd retorted. "I'm not police. Consultant, remember?"

"In that case I'd like to talk to your contact."

"Sorry," Floyd said. "Can't say I'd welcome the competition!"

"Don't be so petty," said the Blue Shadow. "This is bigger than just one man. This is about saving the world and ridding it of the evil that's befallen us."

"Sorry," Floyd repeated. "Can't be done! See you."

He turned to go. The Blue Shadow whipped out, grabbing his arm and twisting it behind his back. The other hand was placed under his chin, forcing him to stare up at the sky as the would-be hero applied pressure to his throat.

"Why don't we try this again," the Blue Shadow suggested mildly.

Floyd drove his free elbow into his captor's ribs, and then kicked behind him. The Blue

Shadow loosened his grip in surprise, and Floyd freed himself, whirling around to face his opponent and continue on fairer ground.

"Easy, little fellow," the Blue Shadow said, taking a step back. "I'm not the villain here."

"Really?" Floyd retorted. "Take your mask off."

"Excuse me?"

"Take off your mask. Let's see who you really are inside there. I bet one of the Lollipop Gang put you up to this, didn't they? That lot gets on my nerves so much."

"I am *not* a villain," the Blue Shadow said. "You on the other hand—"

"Oh stop trying," Floyd said, rolling his eyes. "I'm leaving now. Don't touch me, or I'll break your wrist."

"Very well," the Blue Shadow said with a slight bow. "Perhaps I will see you around, Jeffry Lewis Floyd."

"Perhaps not," Floyd retorted.

THERE'S NO SUCH THING
AS SUPERHEROES

"Paperwork," Inspector Blakely of the Human Resource Department said, folding his hands serenely behind his head and gazing at the ceiling, "Is the glue which holds any organization together. Paperwork, although universally hated, is the method by which departments communicate with each other, without fear of miscommunication. Therefore, no matter how strong the temptation—"

"You're still mad about that whole Emergency Supervillain Task Force thing, aren't you," Adams interrupted. Some part of him that was still meek and respectful showed mild surprise at this attitude towards a superior, but the part of him that still hoped for a promotion had realized that the respectful and obedient rarely get noticed.

"While your actions during that crisis were exemplary, there was still a certain element of chaos present," Blakely said, pursing his lips in annoyance. "If you would like a positive review this quarter I recommend that you—"

"I don't," Adams said. "Now, if you would like me to actually complete any of this precious paperwork then you should really stop interrupting me while I'm in the middle of it."

Blakely was speechless, and Adams smiled beatifically. "Have a nice day, Inspector," he said. "It's always a pleasure seeing you."

Blakely attempted to say something and finally gave up the effort, stalking out with as much dignity as he could muster.

On the way he brushed past something extremely tall and blue.

"Excuse me sir," it said, stepping out of the way.

"Hmph," Blakely said, avoiding treading on its cape.

The Blue Shadow swept into Adams' office.

"Excuse me, sir?" he asked.

Adams looked up.

And up a bit more.

He rubbed his eyes and looked again.

"If you're looking for Floyd, he's out," he said finally. "And I sincerely hope that's good enough for you, because if you start tearing things up in here there will be the devil to pay. By which I mean you will be paying."

"I don't understand," the Blue Shadow stammered politely. "I have seen Mr. Floyd already, which is how I knew to come to you. I have no intention of tearing up—anything."

"What's your name?" Adams demanded.

"The Blue Shadow."

"Blue Shadow, Blue Shadow," Adams mumbled to himself, looking through the stack of notes Floyd had left on his desk. "Nothing about you here. When did you see him?"

"About half an hour ago, sir."

Adams glance sharpened. "Are you working with Metallica?"

"Metallica?" the Blue Shadow's voice rose in indignation. "I would never work with such a villain."

"If he's a villain," Adams demanded, "Then what are you?"

"A hero, sir. Of course."

"There's no such thing as heroes," Adams replied automatically.

"There's no such thing as *super*heroes," Brandon created. "I believe that it is within all of us to be heroes and stand up against the evil which has overtaken us."

Adams blinked a few times. As he processed this. "Take off your mask," he ordered.

"Sir?"

"This isn't a comic book," he stated.

The Blue Shadow obeyed, revealing a face of near-perfect proportions, smooth and chiseled, with bright blue eyes, honest as a child's.

"What is your name?" Adams asked. "Your real name, given to you by your parents at the time of your birth."

"Brandon Reece," he said.

"Sit," Adams ordered. "I have to think this through."

"What is there to think through?" Brandon asked, a slight smile coming to his face. "Is it so unusual to see someone willing to stand up against the evil that rules this city?"

"Evil doesn't rule this city," Adams corrected. "Chaos does. Evil is just a contributing factor."

Brandon bowed his head. "As you wish."

"I want to hear about this meeting you had with Floyd," Adams said. "He was supposed to be defeating Metallica. Is he all right?"

"The last time I spoke to him he was alive and well."

"And the supervillain?"

"He escaped."

"Hmph," Adams said. "I suppose there's a reason for that…"

"Yes," Brandon said, stiffening. "That is one of the things I wish to discuss with you."

"What is?"

"Your consultant allowed the villain to escape," Brandon said. "His behavior was— disturbing. He showed genuine camaraderie with the monster he was supposedly there to destroy and indignation that I stepped in."

"So?" Adams said, spreading his hands. "What does that have to do with the price of tea in China?"

"Nothing, sir," Brandon said, taken aback. "I only wished to confirm that he was who he claimed to be and not a supervillain himself."

"And what if he was?" Adams asked. "What would you do about it?"

"Sir, I have sworn to devote my life to eliminating this pestilence. If Mr. Floyd is a supervillain I consider it my duty to hunt him down and destroy him."

"Brandon, you've given me no reason to trust you or offer you assistance in hunting down pests in this city," Adams said, bowing his head back over his papers in dismissal. "Directing accusations at my consultant, however subtle you think you're being, is not a good way to start building relations."

"I apologize," Brandon said, drawing his cloak around him. "I did not intend offense."

"Let's start over," Adams said. "What do you want?"

"Consider this a courtesy call to let you know of my activities," Brandon said, standing. "I do not wish to be labeled a vigilante or accosted by well meaning police in pursuit of my duties."

"What people label you is not under my control and if you don't want to be 'accosted' by police then don't break the law," Adams said. "Anything else?"

Brandon hesitated, shrugging his broad shoulders and searching helplessly for words. "I wish I had not earned your animosity so early," he said at last. "I was hoping to find more support for my efforts."

Adams sighed and set down his pen, rubbing his eyes again. Blast Blakely and his paperwork—he needed to get more sleep.

"Here's some free advice," he offered. "Ditch the costume. All it does it attract unwanted attention."

"With all due respect, sir, it's a symbol of who I am and what I fight for."

"You look like a supervillain," Adams said bluntly. "Either that or a lunatic."

"I apologize," Brandon said, apparently meaning it. "Part of my mission is to change the belief of people that heroes—"

"Mr. Reece," Adams interrupted. "You are an idealist. I can respect that. If you want to get yourself killed fighting villainy in London then feel free to do so with my blessing. But as a courtesy to me, please, if you see Floyd again, turn and walk away. He doesn't need you stomping all over his hunting grounds and he won't appreciate your heroic attitude."

"I can make you no promises," Brandon said with a slight bow. "But I will do my best."

"Good," Adams said. "Thank you. If there's nothing else—"

"Of course sir."

‹ ‹ ‹

Some time later Floyd turned up, constantly glancing over his shoulder.

"It's all clear," Adams said. "Blakely's already come and gone."

"Oh good," Floyd said in relief. "He's been badgering me about my private investigator's license."

"You don't have one," Adams pointed out.

"I know."

"And you're not an investigator."

"I know!"

"That's his method of teasing," Adams explained.

Floyd blinked. "I didn't think he was capable of it," he said finally.

"Mmm," Adams agreed. "How was your morning?"

"Wasted," Floyd said, flinging himself into a chair. "Metallica got away."

Adams blinked. "Floyd, you have got to stop dancing a tango with that guy and just kill him already."

"What?" Floyd spluttered. "What makes you think—"

"You let him walk, didn't you?"

"It's more complicated then that. This guy showed up and—"

"And you told the villain 'rematch' and let him walk," Adams accused.

Floyd sighed and stopped trying to deny it. "Maybe."

Adams felt his headache coming back and tried to fend it off long enough to force some patience into his voice. "Metallica is a murderer," he explained. "He's one of the most dangerous villains in this city."

"I know."

"So why isn't he dead yet?"

Floyd opened his mouth and shut it again.

"Just because he is polite and amiable doesn't make him any less of a villain," Adams pointed out. "You're just playing games with him for the sport of it!"

Floyd put his face in his hands.

Adams sighed. "Floyd, if you have your reasons, just tell me."

Floyd shrugged and switched to staring at the ceiling. "He plays by the rules," he said. "He amuses me. He's predictable. It's fun. I don't have any other reasons."

"Just kill him already."

"I will."

"Good."

Silence.

Adams decided not to beat around the bush. "I met Brandon Reece."

"Who?"

"The Blue Shadow."

"Oh, him." Floyd made a noise of derision. "Did you send him packing?"

"I told him if he wanted to get himself killed he could do so with impunity."

Floyd sighed.

"Well, he may."

"He's gotten in my way once already," Floyd complained.

"And he's going to do it again," Adams said. "Just be polite. It builds character."

"He thinks he's a superhero," Floyd grouched.

"I know."

"He let Metallica escape."

"He tells it differently."

"Joseph—"

"People like these, they're drifters," Adams interrupted. "They come to a town, stay for a while, and then go somewhere more in need of their 'services.' So just stay out of his way and keep cool, okay?"

"Joseph," Floyd repeated.

"Please," Adams said. "I'm up to my ears in paperwork for this new department and I've got Blakely on my case every single morning, nagging about one thing or another, and I don't want to have to arbitrate between you and a young idealist on top of it. So just play nice and keep it civil, please?"

"You're right, I'm sorry," Floyd apologized. "I can deal with my own problems."

"Do you know how to catch Metallica?" Adams asked, changing the subject.

"Yup," Floyd said, dragging himself to his feet. "I destroyed his battle suit. So he's going to go for supplies."

Adams watched him worriedly. "You're going now?"

"What's wrong with now?"

"You look exhausted."

"It's now or never," Floyd said, conjuring up a grin. "If I don't catch him en route I'll miss my chance."

"Be careful," Adams said, more sharply then he meant to.

"Don't coddle me," Floyd snapped in return. "I can handle myself."

Adams started to snap back, but caught himself and swallowed his anger. "I know you can," he said. "I just—I worry."

Floyd's annoyance evaporated like mist on a sunny morning. He stared very fixedly at a spot on the wall behind Joseph and said, very softly: "And I appreciate it."

"Good," Adams growled. "Now get out of my hair and don't show your face again until Metallica is dead."

Floyd smiled inadvertently, and took his leave.

JUSTICE, MERCY, AND WITTY BANTER

Wireless was the general IT guy for half of London's more technically inclined supervillains. The other half resorted to human technicians, their own henchmen, or inadequate equipment. Some ended up using all three, before finally picking up the phone and dialing the illegal, heavily encrypted number that directed them to the most talented engineer in the country, or possibly the world.

Wireless's superpower involved being able to imagine a device, and have it work perfectly on the first try. He could see solutions to insoluble problems, as long as they involved circuits and wires. He could power electric devices by touching them, hence his moniker. He charged a hefty fee for his services and worked out of many bases around the city. Many supervillains had tried to secure his exclusive services, but their kidnapping attempts ended badly, and usually cost them the functionality of anything more advanced then a screwdriver.

The one person Wireless could never completely avoid was Floyd. The Defender followed him doggedly from lair to lair until he'd worked out all his secret hiding places, could guess his next moves, and could sabotage his most perfect designs. In short, Floyd was the crossed wires in every one of Wireless's brilliant plans.

Floyd found him on his first try, in a lab he'd set up in an abandoned subway tunnel. He found his way through a maze of deadly electric traps without error, and snuck up behind Wireless as the latter peered through a magnifying glass at a delicate piece of circuitry.

"Boo," he said.

Wireless didn't even twitch. "I heard you traipsing around back there," he said, affecting a bored accent. "What do you want?"

His voice was as thin as he was. He had long slender fingers and shoulder length almost-white hair. He was wearing clear goggles and peering intently at his current project.

"I just stopped in to say hi," Floyd said, peering over his shoulder. "What are you working on?"

"Word on the rumor net is that Metallica's battle suit is out of commission," Wireless said, keeping his voice soft. "I'm expecting him in about thirty minutes to pick up a controller for it."

He set down the soldering iron and looked up. "But you knew that already, didn't you."

Floyd smiled in a way that wasn't entirely unpleasant. "Clear out," he suggested. "We're going to need the space."

"I really wish you wouldn't," Wireless said, glancing around. "Some of this equipment is extremely valuable."

"Even better," Floyd said. "You have two options. Leave alive or stay dead. Your choice."

Wireless hesitated.

"Seriously?" Floyd asked, rolling his eyes. "You have to *think* about it?"

"I don't know if you'd really kill me," Wireless said, licking his lips nervously. "You haven't before."

"If I could take your tech off the street a lot of supervillains would suddenly be a lot less dangerous," Floyd said. "You're only barely more valuable to me alive then dead, and I'm serious about taking out Metallica."

Wireless's pale blue eyes flashed in indignation but he kept his voice carefully neutral.

"I'm not going to let this go," he said. "You'll be hearing from me."

"Sure," Floyd said. "Out."

Still glowering, Wireless threw some gear into a backpack and vanished into the tunnels. Floyd took a quick look around the lab, noted the location of some useful tools, and settled back to wait.

Right on schedule Metallica showed up, lugging a heap of wreckage Floyd recognized as part of his battle suit, and looking around for someone.

"Oh," he said, his glance setting on Floyd. "You're not Wireless."

"Nope," Floyd said. "He had to run a quick errand."

"I see," Metallica said, looking around. "You found me rather quickly."

"I keep track of all of Wireless's clients," Floyd explained. "I knew who you'd go to for repairs."

"Ah," Metallica said. "I should have thought of that."

"Probably," Floyd agreed.

"You want to do this now, then?" Metallica asked, looking around for a suitable weapon.

"Unless you want to be interrupted again I suggest we take this opportunity while we have it," Floyd suggested.

"Ah, well, in that case," Metallica agreed, dumping his suit. "Give me a minute?"

"Sure," Floyd said amicably.

The villain pulled two pieces of rusty metal out of the wreckage and began wiring them together. Floyd poked through some of the remnants while he was waiting, and came up with display that glowed bright blue for a second and faded out.

"This is some really nice stuff," he said appreciatively. "Wireless does good work."

"The best," Metallica said, with a hint of pride. "He's protected, you know."

"No, I didn't," Floyd said. "Who then?"

"What's it worth to you?" Metallica asked, hesitating.

"A name?" Floyd said. "Not much. I can find out on my own without hardly any effort. I only asked out of curiosity."

"A day's truce," Metallica offered. "Let me put this back together." He gave his suit a kick.

"Sorry," Floyd said. "I'm tired and I want to go home."

He shook the display and it stayed lit up permanently. Metallica paused in his makeshift construction to come over and look.

"You're not bad yourself," he complimented.

"It's a hobby," Floyd said, and hit him without looking.

The villain slid halfway across the flood before coming to a stop. He glared at Floyd angrily.

"I wasn't ready!" he shouted.

Floyd shrugged. "I was."

He leaped, the villain rolled, a coil of wire toppled off the stack of wreckage and entangled them both. Floyd fought free first, but the villain used his own entrapment to trip him up again. Metallica freed himself enough to reach for the contraption he'd been working on, which turned out to be a primitive ray gun. Purple light briefly illuminated the tunnel, and cut through another wreckage pile, which creaked ominously. Floyd glanced up on it in panic, and gave up on getting out of the wire. He leaped to one side, bringing the annoying coil with him as the stack toppled and fell.

The noise drowned out any other sound, and leaving behind a dust cloud that completely obscured the tunnel. After about five minutes the opponents could hear each other coughing, and Metallica shot again. Floyd reacted, forgetting about the wire still wrapped around his feet. He fell, but jumped forward as he did, bringing the villain down with him. Both grappled for control of the ray gun.

"Your reactions are sluggish," Metallica grunted, stubbornly hanging on.

"It's been a long day," Floyd said, levering for a better hold.

"It's annoying when you don't do your best," the villain said.

"Well, you won't be around much longer to be annoyed," Floyd said consolingly.

The gun split with a loud snap. Floyd stared at the piece in his hand. It was glowing.

"That looks bad," he observed.

An explosion rocked the tunnel, and a bad smell filled the air. Once again the two found each other by the sound of their coughs.

"It was bad," Floyd said, as though it needed confirmation, and threw something. It was large and round and heavy and Metallica dodged it.

It struck something obscured by the smelly smog. The something said: "oof."

Floyd and Metallica stared at each other.

"Buddy of yours?" Floyd asked.

Metallica shook his head. "You killed them all already," he said, almost plaintively. "One of yours?"

"No," Floyd said, puzzled. "I don't have any—"

A blue-gloved fist descended, knocking the villain out cold. The Blue Shadow turned with a dramatic sweep of his cape, and Floyd dodged his next attempt with a shouted curse.

"What do you think you're doing?" he said, hiding behind a pile of something vaguely resembling wheel rims.

The Blue Shadow glanced at the unconscious villain. "Saving you?" he suggested.

"I was doing just fine!" Floyd said, furious. "What are you even doing here?"

"I was eliminating the threat of this supervillain," Brandon said calmly. "Clearly he is capable of creating technology that could prove a serious threat to humanity and—"

"He doesn't create technology!" Floyd said in frustration. "Wireless creates the technology. This guy just buys it, and I was handling that! You don't know anything, but you think you can just barge in here and interfere with my fight?"

"I tracked this villain from the scene earlier today," Brandon said, bristling. "I am only doing my duty."

"Go do your duty somewhere else," Floyd snapped. "This is my turf."

"I will fight villains wherever they may be," Brandon said, his dark eyes flashing. "No matter who attempts to stop me."

Floyd came out from behind the rubble and approached slowly. "Get out of my way," he said tersely. "And then stay out."

"Who do you think you are?" Brandon asked, placing both fists on his hips in a dramatic gesture. "You are nothing but a meddling nuisance who cavorts with the evil kind. You cannot order my comings and goings."

"I'm not ordering," Floyd said, trying to control his temper. "I'm—strongly suggesting. You don't like me, I don't like you, so we should just agree to stay out of each other's way."

"Then leave now," Brandon said. "I have this situation well in hand."

Floyd spluttered. "You don't—I was—just—" he growled in speechless frustration.

"Your inability to state your case only proves your inadequacy for the task at hand," Brandon said. "I believe this conversation has reached the end of its usefulness. Either leave or don't leave; just stay out of my way."

"That's it," Floyd growled. "You're dead."

Metallica groaned, and sat up. He looked at the standoff and decided he'd had enough. "If you're going to be at this for a while," he said, attempting to shuffle past unnoticed, "I'll just be on my way. I've got a splitting headache and—"

Grabbing his arm, Floyd spun him around and shoved him into the rubble of the wreckage heap. Metallica stared in astonishment at the metal shard piercing his chest, and then stared back up at Floyd as if he couldn't quite believe it. And then he died.

It was sudden, unexpected, and even Floyd seemed surprised that he had done it.

"That was brutal," Brandon said very quietly, his voice deepening. "It is true that the villain needed to die, but there is no honor in such a death."

"That's my life," Floyd snapped. "If you don't have the stomach for it, then go home."

Without another word he spun on his heel and left the tunnel.

THIS TOWN IS ONLY BIG ENOUGH FOR ONE SUPERHERO

It was just after midnight when Floyd emerged above ground, somewhere in the near vicinity of his flat. He checked again to make sure he wasn't being followed—the last thing he needed was supervillains invading his home while he slept. Life was complicated enough without adding to it.

He was expecting to be followed, which was why he never anticipated someone already waiting for him.

He was yanked out of the street and into a dark alley before he could react. Someone much bigger and stronger than he was slammed him into a brick wall and held him there, an arm like forged iron pressed against his throat preventing him from talking—or breathing.

Black spots swam across his vision and he realized that fighting back was a futile endeavor. So he did the smart thing—pretended to pass out. His attacker let him drop to the ground like a sack of flour, but before Floyd could follow through with his plan a foot the size of an anvil was planted on his chest, holding him down.

"I know you're not dead," a voice growled. "So don't try any tricks or funny business."

"Or what?" Floyd wheezed. "You'll, I don't know, strangle me? Break my rib cage?"

"I heard you've been causing some problems for Wireless."

Floyd squinted into the darkness trying to make out who his attacker was, but between the poor lighting and the lack of oxygen flowing to his brain the effort was hopeless.

"Who are you?" he demanded. "Since when do supervillains care about each other?"

The enormous weight crushing his chest suddenly lifted. Floyd managed a single breath before it crashed into his side, kicking him across the alley. He crashed into several dustbins and managed to regain his feet, ignoring the sharp pain that told him he'd probably broken some ribs. Again.

He kept his distance from his attacker, but two shadows appeared behind him blocking him from escaping back into the street. Floyd decided to try tact.

"I don't want to fight," he said, raising both hands cautiously. "It's been a long day. Just tell me what you want, and maybe we can work something out."

"It's too late for that," his attacker said, closing in on him. "You need to be taught a lesson."

"A lesson about what? What did I do? Who are you?"

The villain caught up with him as he tripped over the rubbish in the alley, twisting his arm behind his back and slamming him into the wall again. "My name is the Destroyer," he hissed. "And you need to stop messing with my people."

Floyd tried to twist free, but the villain had a grip like death itself and he was already exhausted from two battles in one day.

"You're the one protecting Wireless," he guessed, stalling for time. "I just heard today—was going to pay you a visit tomorrow—"

His forehead slammed into the wall, which then whirled off on some errand of its own. There was roaring in his ears, and he tasted blood. The wall came back for another visit and then gravity shifted—he was falling. The ground was a nice place to be, solid and predictable. There was a sharp pain in his side, someone yanked him to his feet, and then he was flying.

He didn't try to move again. He checked his orientation—ground beneath him, wall behind him—and put his head on his knees. His survival instincts screamed at him to get up and run but he was too damn tired. He had just convinced himself to fall asleep on the spot when the Destroyer spoke again.

"You're not as tough as they say you are," the villain sneered. "I could kill you right now, and what would you do about it?"

"Come back to life," Floyd mumbled. "S'what I always do."

"You are not worth my time," the Destroyer sniffed, and turned away.

"It was a mistake, you know," Floyd called after him.

On the verge of rejoining his shadowy henchmen the Destroyer paused.

"I know now," Floyd explained. "Whatever you're up to—it's something big. Intimidating me won't work. I will find out your plans and at the worst possible moment I'll show up to ruin them."

"Perhaps I should kill you," the Destroyer suggested, taking a step closer. "I'd like to see that smug grin smeared all over the pavement."

Floyd waved a hand in dismissal. "Go away," he said. "I'm too tired to do this with you."

The Destroyer sniffed and turned away, and bumped into something on his way out. The Destroyer was tall, but the Blue Shadow was taller, and his elegant blue costume left no doubt as to his identity. Floyd swore in three languages when he saw him, struggling to put his feelings into words. Neither party paid any attention to him.

"Excuse me," the Destroyer said, stiffening.

"Not tonight," Brandon said, his tone as formal as ever.

"I don't need your help," Floyd said, surprised he found the energy to be angry. "I certainly don't need you following me around the city picking fights with my targets."

"Your pardon," Brandon said, "but you appear to be unable to fight."

"Don't need to fight," Floyd tried to explain. "Don't need you to interfere."

"Little man," the Destroyer attempted again. "Step out of my way so I may continue about my business."

"You have no business in this town," Brandon countered. "You're a supervillain and as such it is my duty to destroy you."

"I am the Destroyer," he stated, puffing out his chest. "Do not be so hasty to challenge me."

"I do not fear you or your evil deeds," the hero countered.

"Just go away," Floyd practically begged. "He's protecting Wireless. It doesn't matter. It's police work..."

"The police are inadequately prepared to deal with a threat of this magnitude," Brandon said, completely missing the point. "Are you ready to fight me, villain?"

"Please," Floyd said. "I would take it as a personal favor if you would just walk away right now."

"And let this villain live?" Brandon exclaimed.

"And let this villain live," Floyd confirmed.

"Never!"

Floyd sighed again. He thought about standing up, and decided it wasn't worth the effort.

"I do not need your protection," the Destroyer said to Floyd. "Nor do I understand why you would feel the need to plead on my behalf to this buffoon."

"Because he's a superhero," Floyd said. "And he's an idiot, and I don't want to watch you break his neck. I'm too tired for that."

"You admit the outcome then?" the Destroyer asked. He grinned in the darkness, showing a flash of pearly teeth.

"Look," Floyd said. "I don't even know what your superpowers are, let alone your weakness. Until now you've been just a distraction in my peripheral vision. However, thanks to your display tonight, you're my next target. Somehow,

I don't think some guy in a costume is going to be able to simply terminate your existence."

"You would be correct in that assessment," the villain said, nodding at the scene behind him.

Floyd looked up to see Brandon flanked by the two thugs, a pistol held firmly to the side of his head. He swore when he saw it, because he realized he was going to have to stand up after all. He did so, bracing himself against the wall to keep from falling.

"Listen, Destroyer," he said. "Have you ever played Truth or Dare?"

"You're going to play games with this monster?" Brandon shouted, outraged.

"Shut up," said the thugs, the Destroyer, and Floyd—all at the same time.

"Or you'll get yourself shot," Floyd added. He turned his attention back to the Destroyer.

"I am familiar with it, yes," the Destroyer said.

"I have a new version," Floyd said. "I call it Truth or Shadow. First person to tell a lie forfeits the big blue hunk over there."

"You expect me to play by the rules?" The Destroyer asked, raising his eyebrows.

"No," Floyd said, shaking his head. "I'm just stalling for time here."

He struck out at the villain, but the blow had no effect beyond shattering the bones in his hand. He grimaced in pain, ducked and rolled away from the villain's retaliating blow. He knocked the two thugs out of the way before they knew what was coming, grabbed Brandon's arm and sprinted toward the end of the alley.

"This isn't over yet!" the Destroyer roared.

"I know," Floyd shouted back, using the last of his energy to summon a cocky grin. "And now I know your superpower."

It should have ended there. Floyd turned to keep going, but Brandon remained like an anchor.

Floyd swore. "Come on!" he shouted. "We don't have time for this!"

"Then go," Brandon said. "But I am not leaving without putting this sniveling worm in his place."

The henchmen didn't bother getting back up. The Destroyer took a step forward.

"What did you say?" he hissed.

"He didn't say anything," Floyd said. "Let's go."

"You and your kind are a scourge on this planet," Brandon continued. "I will wipe you out of existence like I wipe the dirt from my shoes."

"I don't take well to threats," the Destroyer said with a smile.

"I don't take well to villains," Brandon retorted. "You are a worthless, filthy piece of garbage and I will end you."

"Strong words," the Destroyer said, his smile faltering, "but that's all they are."

"I may not have the means to destroy you now," Brandon returned. "But soon that will not stop me."

"Then why on earth are you standing here making him angry?" Floyd finally broke in. "First rule of threatening your opponent—don't make him angry unless you're ready to fight!"

"Indeed," the Destroyer hissed. "You should listen to the annoying little one there. You have made a grave mistake tonight."

"I don't think so," Brandon said calmly.

"I will make you pay for this," The Destroyer said. "You will suffer as you have never suffered before."

Brandon stepped forward and balled his fists. "Let's get started then," he said.

"Oh, not tonight," the Destroyer said, smiling again. "Not tonight. I have preparations to make."

"Face me!" Brandon shouted.

But the Destroyer gathered his thugs about him and waved. "See you soon," he promised.

And then he was gone.

Floyd's brain finally caught up with his body, his knees gave out under him and he decided to fall. Brandon caught him.

"We need to get you to a hospital," the hero said gravely.

"You too," Floyd retorted. "The special kind."

But the night seemed even darker than usual, the street light flickering in an unusual pattern.

"You're hurt," Brandon said from a great distance. Floyd realized what was happening and started swearing methodically, forcing himself to stay alert.

"You can't," he said finally, in between curse words. "You can't, because I'm not human, and I can't die, and I'll be fine."

Brandon opened his mouth and shut it again. He repeated the motion several times, like a fish. Floyd was so tired he wanted to cry, but he couldn't, not in front of this stranger.

"Brandon," he managed finally, "For the love of life, don't do anything without talking to Joseph."

"Joseph?"

"Sergeant Adams."

"But—"

"He'll tell you the truth."

"I don't know..."

"*Please,*" Floyd whispered. He thought about standing up and walking home, but the mere idea made him black out for a moment, and when he came to the alley was full of flashing blue lights.

Joseph touched his forehead and said: "Are you okay?"

He wasn't, he really wasn't, but he just said: "I've only been out for ten seconds."

"Forty minutes," Adams corrected. "Come on, I'll take you home."

"Brandon," Floyd said. "He did something stupid...'sgoing to get himself killed..."

"I know," Adams said, getting an arm under Floyd's shoulder. "He told me. I took care of it. You won't have to worry about him anymore."

"What did you do?"

"I hired him."

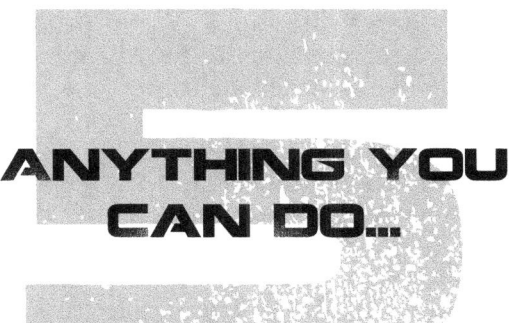

ANYTHING YOU CAN DO...

The human race defines "Superhero" as "a benevolent fictional character with superhuman powers." The rest of the galaxy defines it as "a non-existent entity" with an entry right between "cure for supervillains" and "honest politicians." Floyd had given up on any pretty adjectives, and settled on just plain "idiots."

"Morning, Floyd," Adams said. "Feeling better?"

"Ermph," Floyd said, slumping into his chair. He stared at his computer but didn't turn it on. A moment later he said: "I think I was delirious last night."

"You probably were," Adams agreed. "I'm sorry you had to go through all that."

"Turns out the Destroyer is protecting Wireless," Floyd offered. "Diligently. He's up to something."

"He's the one who beat you up?"

"Mmm," Floyd said. "Like I said, he doesn't want anyone messing around with Wireless."

"So what's he up to?"

Floyd shrugged. "Search me," he said. "I just thought I'd mention it in case you hear anything."

"I'll try to pay attention," Adams promised.

It was a moment before Floyd said anything else. "I could have been delirious," he said, "Or dreaming. But last night, I could swear you told me you'd hired Brandon Reece."

"Oh yes," Adams said. "I did."

Floyd dropped the pencil. "You did?" he repeated. "You did what?"

"I also told him about you. Apparently you assured him I would tell him the truth, and I wanted to make sure he didn't misinterpret anything you said."

"I didn't—," Floyd gasped, "I mean, I did but—but I didn't mean to. I was just—"

"I know," Adams said, raising one hand. "It's all right. Like I said, I straightened it out."

"By *hiring* him?"

"Yes."

"You're replacing me," Floyd said, throwing up his hands. "You're taken in by this flashy law-abiding newcomer. You like how malleable he is; how willing to follow protocol and procedure. You think that if he works out you won't need to keep someone as difficult as me around."

"Don't be childish," Adams said. "I am not replacing you."

"Yes, you are. Why else would you possibly want *two* supervillain hunters to keep in line?"

Adams looked up, blinking. "I don't," he said. "I'm just trying to protect the one I have."

"Oh," Floyd said, suddenly speechless. "Um, thank you?"

Adams smiled. "Is there anything else I can do for you, Mr. Floyd?"

"No," Floyd said, still confused. "I think I'll just—go kill something."

"The Destroyer?"

"No, I don't know anything about him yet. I'm going to get rid of Flamethrower."

"Did you figure out how to kill him?" Adams asked in surprise.

"I'm going to make a trap," Floyd grinned. "Hopefully it will work."

"Check in with me later," Adams said. "Try not to get killed."

"No promises," Floyd said. "And don't wait up for me."

"Fine," Adams grumbled. "Have a good day."

Floyd didn't bother to respond to that.

❮ ❮ ❮

Brandon hadn't been a superhero for very long, but he felt comfortable in the role. He kept himself to a strict regime of sleep, early rising, and healthy, moderate meals. He spent at least three hours a day working out—honing his strength and speed. He would need to be at the top of his game to defeat the evil that plagued the world.

He kept his small motel room clean himself, preferring privacy to service. He made sure his costume was washed and pressed before he went to bed each night, ready for another day of crime fighting. He kept a very nice suit in the closet in case he ever needed to slip into another character. He rose at 6:30 sharp and ate cereal for breakfast, showered, and brushed his teeth. He combed his hair neatly even though no one could see it, dressed, and was down at Scotland Yard by half past seven.

Sergeant Adams looked like he had been there all night. He barely even spared a glance when Brandon presented himself, fully costumed and ready for duty.

"You're early," Adams grunted, barely sparing him a glance. "I thought I told you to come back at nine."

"I like to get started early in the day," Brandon said, and glanced around. "Where's Mr. Floyd?"

"It's just Floyd," Adams said. "And he's working. Why?"

"Wouldn't it be more efficient for you to brief us both at the same time?" he inquired.

Again that strange look. "I don't brief Floyd," Adams said. "He briefs me."

Brandon gave a slight smile. "I thought you were in charge," he said, concealing his uncertainty.

"I am," Adams said. "But I don't tell Floyd what to do. I just help him do it."

Brandon was more puzzled than ever, but he didn't let it show.

"Do you have anywhere specific you'd like me to go?" he asked. "Anything you want me to do? Any public menaces I can disable?"

"Oh yes," Adams said. "Definitely. Just give me a chance to see what Floyd left me last night, all right?"

"Night owl, is he?" Brandon asked, trying to make conversation.

Adams only grunted in reply. He looked first through the papers on his desk, and finally checked his email. Brandon sat quietly in one of the over-sized leather waiting chairs, and tried to be patient.

"Here we go," he said finally. "There's going to be a major jewel heist at nine this morning. You'll need the address—"

"Nine?" Brandon exclaimed. "But it's after eight now!"

"Yes, you'll have to hurry," Adams said. "And when you're done with that—"

"I can't fly, you know," Brandon pointed out indignantly.

"—there are reports of a monster sighting down by the dock. Try not to tear up any historic or very expensive landmarks, please."

Brandon accepted the address and the case files, and stiffly left the room.

❯ ❯ ❯

The Flamethrower had a very nice lair, all things considered. Floyd killed the two door guards, scared off the household staff, disabled every alarm in the place, but left the security cameras running. He poured himself a drink, took care of a few preliminaries, and settled down in a red plush chair to wait.

He didn't have to wait very long; a fact he chalked up to the Flamethrower having a personal alarm that let him know when his home had been broken into.

"You," the villain growled, from the doorway.

Floyd had seen him coming on the security cameras, and was fully prepared. Which meant that he hadn't so much as uncrossed his legs. He leaned back in the red plush chair and smiled up at the ugly face of the Flamethrower.

The Flamethrower had been involved in an accident involving chemicals and radioactivity, and it had permanently scarred his face with a pattern of flames. It was difficult to mistake him for anyone else.

"Glad you could drop in," Floyd said, feigning carelessness. "We need to have a little chat; you and I."

"You're dead," the Flamethrower snarled, and launched a column of flame at Floyd's face.

Floyd tossed the rest of his drink into the villain's face, and scrambled to get out of the way.

"What part of 'talk' do you not understand?" Floyd spluttered, working his way around the room. The Flamethrower systematically destroyed every piece of furniture in the place as Floyd darted behind first one and then the other, keeping up a steady stream of chatter.

"I thought we could settle this peacefully," Floyd said. "Like adults, you know? I give you what you want; you give me what I want."

"You have nothing I want," the villain muttered in his grating voice.

"Oh, is that true?" Floyd said with a grin, darting behind the computer monitors.

A flash of fire arced across the room. Sparks flew everywhere. The security cameras went black. Unexpectedly the lights went out at the same time. For a moment the only sound was Floyd's laughter. The villain shot out randomly in the dark, trying to find him. His flames illuminated the rubble for only a few seconds at a time, worsening the mess and accomplishing nothing. Finally he gave up, and stood silent in the middle of the room, trying to make anything out in the dark. A sulphuric smell filled the air.

"We're underground," Floyd said unexpectedly. "You can't see anything because I rigged the power earlier to run through the computer. So we're completely in the dark unless you can find the door and get out."

The villain started towards it, but stopped when Floyd started laughing again.

"You built this place to be impregnable," he explained. "Your lair is a bomb-shelter. In case of emergency the door seals and it can't be opened again—unless you enter a top-secret code into the computer."

Flamethrower hissed, and shot towards the sound of the voice. Floyd wasn't there.

"You know what else was on the computer?" Floyd asked. "All your evil plans. All your top secret schematics. You don't trust the Internet, so you kept it all locally. Oops. I bet that's lost forever now as well."

"You're dead!" The Flamethrower roared. "Dead!"

"Oh wait," Floyd said, pretending he had just thought of something. "What this? Is this maybe a backup I made before you got here? Why, so it is! I wonder if I should destroy that too?"

The Flamethrower stopped destroying. "What do you want?" he said, in a surprisingly normal tone of voice.

"Oh, I don't know," Floyd said. "I haven't found your weakness yet, so I know I can't kill you. I doubt you'll exchange that for this data; but if I can keep the data and get out alive maybe your secret is on there. Then again, maybe not. You might not know your own weakness. It can be harder to find in physical mutations like yourself."

"Give me the backup and I'll let you walk," the Flamethrower offered.

"There's a problem with that too," Floyd said. "I lost my informant today. My whole plan for defeating you went awry. I can't just walk away from that, because I can't let you hurt more people."

The Flamethrower paused. "How much time do you want?"

"Seven days," Floyd said, and the teasing tone dropped out of his voice. "You want this backup you give me *seven day*s without hurting anyone else."

"Done," the Flamethrower said instantly.

"You know what happens if you lie to me," Floyd said warningly.

"We all know," the Flamethrower snarled. "Maybe I should warn you that you've just given me the time and date you're going to attack. I'll be ready for you, Jeffry Floyd. You won't be able to stop me."

"I'll know your weakness," Floyd said carelessly. "It won't matter what you do. See you later!"

For a moment there was silence.

It stretched on into an audible question mark.

"I don't suppose you brought a computer?" the Flamethrower asked.

"Nope," Floyd admitted.

"So you have no way of opening those impregnable blast doors?"

"That's correct," Floyd said.

"We're stuck here?"

"So it would seem."

"You don't have a plan?"

"No plan," Floyd said cheerfully.

"You're dead," the Flamethrower growled.

"We both are," Floyd pointed out, "Unless you have a backup system."

"Do I look like the sort to have a backup system?" the Flamethrower asked.

"No," Floyd said despondently in the dark.

The silence stretched on and on and on.

"Do you know what your weakness is?" Floyd asked hopefully.

"No," the Flamethrower growled. "And I never want to find out."

"Why not?" Floyd asked. "I mean, doesn't it make you curious? What is the one thing that can stop you? Water doesn't. Liquid nitrogen doesn't. I mean, darn, I've tried everything."

"Shut up," Flamethrower growled.

For a few minutes Floyd did. Then he started chuckling.

"What on earth is so funny?" the Flamethrower asked.

"I remembered what else was run by your computers," Floyd said. "That's been shut down along with everything else."

"What's that?" the villain demanded.

"The ventilation," Floyd explained.

"Very funny," the Flamethrower said. "I would never be that stupid."

"I was here before you, remember," Floyd said. "I routed them through. Keyed everything to shut down when you incinerated your hard drive."

"Why on earth would you do that?" the Flamethrower demanded. "Now we'll both suffocate!"

"You'll suffocate," Floyd corrected. "I don't need to breathe. Much, anyway."

"But you'll still die!" The Flamethrower protested.

"You'll die first," Floyd countered. "And I wonder how your fire will burn? The more you use it the faster the oxygen is gone and—"

"You planned on this?" the Flamethrower said. "What's the point? You still can't get out. It's suicide!"

"If you'd been around longer then you'd know suicide is my modus operandi," Floyd said. "Anyway, I told you I'd find your weakness."

"My weakness is that I need to breathe?" the Flamethrower said incredulously. "Everyone needs to breathe. How is that a weakness?"

"It's a common weakness of all humans," Floyd chuckled. "Not that hard after all, eh?"

"I"m going to kill you," the Flamethrower said, coming to his feet. "If I'm going to die, I'm taking you down with me."

"Eh, I was getting bored anyway," Floyd said. "Catch me if you can!"

The Flamethrower launched flame in the direction of Floyd's voice, but Floyd was no longer there. A mocking laugh hung in the air, and the Flamethrower shot again. On the seventh time across the room Floyd became careless. He tripped over something, stumbled into the wall, and fell. Before he could register the mistake the Flamethrower had caught him. Tendrils of flame wrapped around him, and Floyd screamed.

"Feeling out of breath yet?" the Flamethrower taunted.

Floyd didn't try to answer.

A few minutes later he passed out.

❮   ❮   ❮

Floyd woke up in darkness, the smell of smoke and sulfur thick in the air. He tried to breathe it in and choked, every motion increasing the throbbing pain in his head. His heart was racing with the fear of remembered nightmares. The smoke confused and disoriented him, and he could see nothing in the absolute darkness. The longer he tried to calm down and get his bearings the harder it became. He was suffocating down here. He had to get out.

He struggled to his feet and tripped over something almost immediately. It turned out to be the body of the Flamethrower, his firepower exhausted by the lack of oxygen. Some further part of his plan came to mind and he reached for his pocket—only to discover it wasn't there. Floyd cursed fire-based superpowers everywhere and tried to think. He wouldn't have left himself without a way out. He would have planned for this.

There was a red plush chair in the middle of the room that was the only thing not incinerated by the fire. Floyd reached for it, and found his coat draped over the back. He put it on. In the pocket was a small penlight. The light helped, even though breathing was still an exercise in futility. He returned to the Flamethrower's body and verified that he was dead.

The burns on his arms and torso didn't hurt as badly as he expected. Either he'd been out long enough for them to start to heal already of the Flamethrower had blacked out shortly after Floyd himself. His plan had worked. Now he just had to remember how to get out of an impregnable bomb shelter that could only be opened by a computer he'd destroyed earlier.

In his other pocket was a mobile phone. He turned it on and found out it was close to midnight, and that he had no mobile phone service. In spite of that the phone informed him there was a message waiting.

"This is a computer, moron," it said. "All you have to do is hit enter."

Floyd smiled. "I really am that good," he told himself. The blast doors opened and he stepped into the cool night air.

...I CAN DO BETTER

Floyd wasn't planning on battling Speedy on Friday night, but supervillains run on their own schedule without consulting their opponents. So instead of going home and sleeping after his big battle with the Flamethrower he was lurking around outside of a four-star restaurant, watching Speedy zip around annoying the patrons. He couldn't just walk up to a villain with the power of super-speed and expect anything productive to result, so he started laying a trap.

Predictably, Speedy noticed what he was doing and came zipping out to stop him. Floyd dodged the first attack, and was flattened by the second. Slowly, cautiously, he stood back up and closed his eyes, listening for gentle breeze and would alert him the supervillain was coming back for a third. He took a quick step back when it did, and stuck his foot out.

Tripping a supervillain moving at nearly the speed of light can have amusing results. Speedy hit the ground and tore up the pavement in a wide swath until he crashed into the front of the restaurant, bringing down most of the front wall in the process, finally coming to a halt near the back of the building.

"Damn," Floyd muttered. "I didn't mean for him to go in *that* direction."

The patrons of the restaurant had gone from moderate annoyance at Speedy's tricks to complete outrage. The manager came rushing out breathless, and immediately settled on Floyd, plainly visible through the hole Speedy had made, as a likely scapegoat.

"You!" he shouted in a thick Italian accent. "How dare you? Don't move; I'm going to call the police. Right now I'm going to call the police. This is an outrage! This is—is terrible!"

He was shaking with fury as his patrons heaped insults on his head and flooded out through the demolished front wall. In the chaos Floyd lost sight of Speedy, on the other side of the crowd.

The villain had also moved from mere annoyance with Floyd into the land of murderous rage. He zipped back through the crowd, literally blowing people out of his way in order to kick the Defender of the Earth firmly into a building on the other side of the road. Floyd hit the wall, which became dented but remarkably remained standing, and fell. He wondered idly, as he tried to stand, how many bones he'd broken this time. He glanced up to see Speedy standing over him, finally visible since he wasn't actually moving. He was grinning instead, waiting to see if Floyd was actually going to manage to stand or not.

Floyd reached out for the wall to steady him—and missed. Speedy laughed, a high keening sound that came out far too fast to sound human. He said something too, a taunt of some kind, but it was equally unintelligible. Floyd caught his breath and glared up at him. Someone had suddenly appeared behind the villain—someone ridiculously tall and very blue. Speedy raised his booted foot aimed at Floyd's unbroken leg at the same time that the shadow raised both hands over his head. Floyd rolled out of the way as the villain collapsed under the crushing blow. He glanced up at the superhero in surprise and then reached over to the villain to check for a pulse.

There was none. He grunted in approval.

"Are you all right?" the Blue Shadow asked formally.

"You broke his neck," Floyd said, dodging the question. "You're not too bad at this supervillain thing."

"It is unfortunate," the Blue Shadow said. "I did not intend to kill him."

Floyd raised his eyebrows. "You intended to let him live so he could sneak up behind you and kill you instead?" he asked.

"He has committed no crimes that I know of worthy of death."

"He was moving faster than a human being can," Floyd countered. "That's worthy of death."

"Without evidence it is not my place to judge," Brandon said. "To do so would make me as much a monster as they."

"If you lose that attitude," Floyd said, rolling his eyes, "You might actually be pretty good at this gig."

"You are fortunate I came along at that moment," the Blue Shadow said in a grave tone of voice.

"Yes," Floyd begrudged. "I suppose I am."

He gave up on moving, and tried to ignore the twisting, gut-wrenching pain of broken bones in multiple parts of his body.

"Do you require assistance?" the Blue Shadow asked.

Floyd shook his head. "I'll just sit here until everything magically fixes itself," he said, with a weak attempt at humor. "Thanks for your help with Speedy."

"Speedy? That's what you called him?"

Annoyance mingled with the pain on Floyd's face. "Seriously?" he said. "Why does everyone criticize? It gets the point across, right?"

"It's just so—" the Blue Shadow chose his word carefully, "—inelegant."

"Who cares about elegance?" Floyd demanded. "They're supervillains. It's all blood and chaos and slaughter and misery."

He slumped back against the dented wall and closed his eyes in exhaustion.

"And yet, there is a certain beauty to them as well, don't you think?"

"No. I don't."

"They have to exist for something," the superhero mused. "Surely such a phenomena couldn't spring into existence without some purpose in mind. Surely—"

"They exist to perpetrate evil deeds," Floyd interrupted. "Isn't that deep enough for you?"

"Let me take you back to Scotland Yard," the Blue Shadow offered abruptly. "Your friend can take care of your wounds and you can rest in comfort."

"They're not wounds," Floyd growled. "They're broken bones, and it will hurt more to move them then to just sit here all night. Don't you have something else to be doing other than harassing me?"

"Brandon?" a new voice entered the conversation. "Is everything all right?"

Floyd opened his eyes and stared in wonder at the vision that presented itself. The newcomer was tall and blond and slender. A slinky grey evening gown clung to her like a second skin; a slit up the left side allowed her to walk. Her head actually came up to Brandon's shoulder, and she stood next to him possessively, one hand holding firmly onto his arm while the other clutched a small, spangled handbag.

"Hello," Floyd said from his pile of dust and rubble. "Who in the universe are you?"

Brandon coughed nervously. "Jeffry Floyd," he said nervously, "Allow me to present my fiancée—Jane Maurice."

Floyd started to laugh, disguised it as a cough, and composed himself.

"I'm sorry," he said. "Could you repeat that? I thought you said....your fiancée."

"I did."

"Oh," Floyd said. "You did." And then he started laughing.

"Who is this?" Jane asked, glancing at him the way one glances at a stray dog. "And what is wrong with him?"

"He's a consultant for Scotland Yard," Brandon said. "Don't mind his manners—I expect it's just pent up stress. He's in a great deal of pain."

Jane's irritation smoothed instantly into sympathy. Evening gown not withstanding she crouched down next to Floyd and cupped his face in her hands. "Are you hurt very badly?" she asked. "I'm sure Brandon can take you to a hospital, if you need it. We have a car parked a few blocks away."

"Let me guess," Floyd said. "Where Brandon goes trouble follows so you park the car far enough away that it won't end up as collateral damage. Very cute, both of you."

Jane frowned. "You know my fiancée—"

"Professionally," Floyd said, cutting her off. "We're both consultants at Scotland Yard. Which is to say, the city pays us to beat up bad guys."

He gestured, and Jane noticed the supervillain's body for the first time. She pulled away from it in distaste, and Brandon helped her straighten up.

"You're sure you're all right?" Brandon asked.

"Fine," Floyd said, gesturing negligently. "Now let me ask you something."

Brandon frowned distrustfully. "What's that?"

"I know you and I have had our differences," Floyd said in preface. "But you stand for chivalry and honor and—and elegance. So I think you'll agree with me when I say—what the hell do you think you're doing?"

Brandon recoiled as if he'd been slapped. "Excuse me?"

"She's beautiful and gentle and kind and understanding and perfect," Floyd practically spat. "You—you kill supervillains! You're a target! You park your car several blocks away to avoid it getting damaged and then keep your most priceless possession directly in the line of fire! Are you an idiot or are you just that arrogant?"

"I know what sort of danger I face," Jane said, smoothly intercepting Brandon's retort. "I take certain measure to protect myself should a situation arise."

"And what if you fail?" Floyd demanded. "What if you get killed or captured?"

"That's my risk to take."

"And you let her take it?" He turned back to Brandon.

"Jane saved my life," Brandon said. "She gives me the motivation to do what I do. Without her—I would not have been here to save your life tonight."

"Do you love her?" Floyd demanded.

Brandon was taken aback. "I don't see how that—"

"Do you love her?" he repeated insistently.

"Yes, I do."

"More than you love anything else in this world? More than life? More than safety?"

"Not that it's any of your business—but yes."

"And yet you put your *happiness* above her safety?" Floyd accused.

"It's my choice," Jane interjected. "I won't leave him."

"Then you are both idiots," Floyd said, "And you're both going to end up dead because of it."

"Not this again," Brandon sighed. "I just saved your life."

"I would have come back if you hadn't," Floyd said. "You don't have that luxury."

"Even if that's true—"

"If you love her, you'll stay as far away from her as possible," Floyd said. "That's all I've got to say on the subject."

"You're just jealous," Brandon sneered. You just can't handle it that not everyone is as lonely and miserable as you are. You think that because you're an outcast we all should be? Maybe girls don't go for the whole "alien from outer space" thing, but not all of us have that problem!"

"Let's just go, Brandon," Jane said uneasily.

"Yeah, make fun of me," Floyd said. "But being lonely has it's perks. At least I won't have the blood of my dearest love on my hands."

"Is that a threat?"

"It's a prediction."

Brandon balled his hands into fists and took a step forward. "I swear, if you weren't already down—"

Floyd reached for the wall and hauled his feet under him. His broken leg buckled under the weight and the pain almost made him black out, but he gritted his teeth and fought through it.

"Go ahead," he said quietly. "You were saying?"

"Let's go," Jane practically begged, clinging to Brandon's arm. "Don't fight with this man, Brandon. It's just words."

"Sticks and stones," Floyd taunted. "But they won't be mere words anymore when you have to bury her. Because you'll be the one to kill her, Brandon."

"I would never—"

"When she dies it will be your fault," Floyd said. "If you continue on this path. You can't have both, Brandon. You can't be a superhero and a husband."

"That's what this all comes down to," Brandon said with a sigh, relaxing. "This is all about trying to get me to give up my life's work."

"No!" Floyd shouted in frustration. "I gave up trying to save your life last week. If you want to fight supervillains feel free. I won't stop you. But Jane—she's a decent girl. She deserves better then to be tortured to death for no reason then because she's acquainted with a known supervillain hunter!"

Brandon offered his arm to Jane. "Shall we go, dear?"

Jane slipped her hand through it easily, but threw a glance back at Floyd.

"I'm sorry you've never been in love," she said quietly. "If you had—you would understand."

Floyd started to answer and shut his mouth without saying anything. He sagged back against the wall and watched them leave. Jane's silver gown was the last thing to be swallowed by the blackness, and moments later he heard her scream.

MEA CULPA

Floyd ran.

Blind, murderous pain exploded like fireworks in his mind but he didn't have time for things like pain or common sense or not moving on a broken leg. He ran.

He ran towards the sound of Jane's scream, and the muffled sounds of physical combat. It was only a few feet, but it felt like forever. He saw in a single glance what had happened, how the henchmen had waited in the dark shadows surrounding their car and jumped them when they approached. Jane lay on the ground, blood staining her slinky evening gown. Brandon fought valiantly, but he was unarmed and could barely hold his own. Floyd collapsed at Jane's side, turning her onto her back and checking for a pulse. There was blood on her head and she was unconscious but breathing. He turned his attention back to the fight.

There were seven henchmen. Brandon had already disabled two of them. They were still and unmoving—perhaps dead. A third was alive, but unable to stand. The other four were holding the superhero down as an eighth figure approached out of the bushes.

Floyd recognized the red suit and dark hair, even in the dark. He kept silent.

The Destroyer sneered at Brandon, and yanked the mask off so he could stare into his naked face.

"You thought you could belittle and insult me," he hissed. "Now you will learn how weak you humans truly are."

He gestured to the henchmen who let go of Brandon and started towards Floyd and Jane.

"No!" Brandon shouted, but a single blow from the Destroyer knocked him senseless. Floyd lunged towards the first of the approaching henchmen, but his body betrayed him and he fell short.

"Floyd, Floyd, Floyd," the Destroyer chuckled. "Why, you should be thanking me. I'm doing you a favor, after all, taking this little irritant of your hands. Soon the city will be yours again. Just the way you like it, right?"

"I don't know what you mean," Floyd blustered.

"Tell your rival, when he wakes up, that if he wishes to see his girl alive again, then he'll come to me alone and unarmed tomorrow at midnight, Belmont View."

"You'll kill him," Floyd said. "Why would he do that?"

"Weren't you listening?" the villain laughed. "He's in love. That's why."

Then he disappeared, taking Jane with him.

Floyd dragged himself over to Brandon, shaking him in the dark. The hero groaned foggily.

"Jane?" he asked.

"They took her," Floyd said in a harsh whisper. "But we're going to get her back, okay? He gave me a rendezvous."

"Who did?"

"The Destroyer. Come on, let's get back to Scotland Yard. Adams will help us make a plan."

"Us?" Brandon sat up, rage in his eyes. "There is no us, *Mr.* Floyd. You've never been interested in working together before and—"

"And I'm sorry," Floyd interrupted. "Let's try this again. I respect your abilities and your decision to devote your life to fighting supervillains. I was only opposed to you because of my own fear and insecurity. Please accept my humblest apologies and work with me to *save a life.*"

"This is all a set-up," Brandon growled. "You're just trying to prove your point from earlier."

"You're being paranoid," Floyd said patiently. "Listen to me, Brandon. Jane is going to die. They're going to murder her. Unless—"

"Yes?" Brandon said eagerly, latching onto the word. "Unless what? What did they tell you, Floyd? What does the Destroyer want?"

"We can get her back," Floyd said, dodging the question. "You and me. I know where he's taking her. We can get some backup and sneak in and rescue her and no one has to die."

"What does he want, Floyd?" Brandon raged.

"Brandon—"

"I'm not going to play games with Jane's life because of your arrogance!" he shouted. He grabbed Floyd by the collar and slammed him against the car, eliciting a hiss of pain. "Tell me what the Destroyer wants! Tell me!"

"He wants you!" Floyd shouted in return.

For a moment no one said anything.

"He wants you," Floyd repeated, more quietly. "Because of how you humiliated him the other day. He wants you to walk into his lair and surrender yourself and then he wants to do unspeakable things to your mind and body. And you'll do whatever he asks because right across the room from you you'll see Jane—and anytime you refuse he'll hurt her instead. And finally, right in the moment before you die, when you can barely keep your eyes open and your thoughts together, he'll slit her throat so that he can see the expression on your face when you realize it was all pointless. *That's* what he wants, Brandon."

Brandon thought about this for long enough that Floyd decided it was safe to breathe.

"Take me back to Scotland Yard," he said, "And we'll get that backup I talked about."

"I have to go to him," Brandon said.

"What?"

"The Destroyer. I have to go to him. I have to give him what he wants."

"Are you insane?" Floyd shouted. "Did you not hear a word I said? If you go he'll kill you."

"If I don't go he'll kill Jane."

"He's going to kill her anyway! Don't you see that? Don't be an impulsive, irrational, idiotic—" he struggled to come up with a suitable epithet and abandoned the effort. "You're not thinking straight," he finished finally. "Come back to the station with me and we'll figure something out."

"Where?" Brandon asked, breathless from something other than exercise. "Where and when?"

"Brandon, please—"

"Where and when?" he repeated, shaking him. "Where and when?"

"I'm not going to tell you," Floyd protested. "I'm not going to let you go rushing into your death without properly—"

The sentence cut off abruptly as Brandon's fist connected with his sternum, dropping the smaller man like a sack of flour.

Floyd gasped in pain as he landed on his broken ribs. He curled up around himself as the assault continued.

"Where?" Brandon demanded, kicking him viciously. "When? Tell me, Floyd! Or so help me—"

A whimper escaped Floyd, and the sound seemed to bring Brandon to his senses. He dropped down on his knees beside him, guilt edging into his voice.

"Aw, come on Floyd," he said, putting a hand on his shoulder. "I don't want to do this. Just tell me what I need to know."

Floyd reached into his pocket and fulled out his mobile phone. The glass was webbed with cracks, and the display flickered unreliably. With a whispered curse he dropped it. He gestured to Brandon who leaned in close, hoping to get the information he wanted so desperately.

"Call Joseph," Floyd whispered. "Please."

And then he lost the battle to pain.

❮ ❮ ❮

When he came to he was lying in bed, at home. Someone had splinted his leg, and wrapped his ribs up tightly. The angle of the sunlight told him it was late afternoon. Most of the pain had dulled to a minor complaint, but when he tried to stand his broken leg screamed and he lost his balance and fell. He stood again, more carefully, and tried to pretend that if he ignored the pain it would go away.

It didn't, but he made a good pretense. On the table that balanced precariously between kitchen and sitting room there was a new phone, and a note. The note said "Call me." It was unsigned.

Floyd sat down, and pressed 1. It rang straight through to Adams desk.

"Oh, good, you're up," the Sergeant said. "Is there anything I should know?"

"I need a ride," Floyd said. "I can't walk there on this leg."

"Yeah, but what happened to you?"

"Long story. Come pick me up and I'll tell you."

There was a muffled conversation on the other side of the phone. "Floyd..."

"Have you seen Brandon?" he blurted out.

"I'll be there in twenty minutes," Adams said, and hung up. Floyd got dressed and scrounged for some weapons, and went outside to wait for him.

The drive back to the station was silent. Floyd didn't volunteer any information and Adams didn't ask. When they walked into Adams' office together, Brandon was already waiting. He stood when they entered. He was in full costume, but the mask was crunched up in a ball in his left hand. He wore an expression of painful regret, but Floyd met his eyes stonily and turned away.

Adams gestured to chairs and sat behind his desk.

"All I know," he said, "is that you, Floyd, have some information Brandon needs. Now if I hear you two have been fighting again—"

"I fought with Speedy," Floyd interrupted. "He threw me into a building."

"And?" Adams prompted.

"And then Jane was kidnapped by the Destroyer."

"Who's Jane?"

"His fiancée."

"My fiancée," Brandon said at the same time.

"Your fiancée?" Adams said, outraged. "Are you insane?"

"That's what I said," Floyd mumbled smugly.

"My personal life—" Brandon started.

"No, he's right," Adams interrupted. "You said you wanted to fight supervillains. You didn't say anything about dragging another person along with you!"

"Jane is not being dragged into anything," Brandon said stiffly. "I can protect her."

"The only way to protect her is to keep her in another city, or a cave somewhere," Adams said. "Never let her out in the daylight, never be seen in public together. You're a superhero, for crying out loud, Brandon. I'm just surprised this didn't happen sooner."

"Thank you," Floyd said emphatically.

"Shut up," Adams snapped. "What's done is done. You said Jane was captured by the Destroyer. Do you know where she's being held?"

"Yes," Brandon said stiffly. "That's what Floyd is refusing to reveal."

"Floyd?"

"The Destroyer wants him to surrender," Floyd said. "Brandon intends to do so. If I tell him where she is they'll both die."

"Floyd," Adams said, very gently.

"I have a right to know," Brandon said stiffly. "Jane is my responsibility, and I will do what I deem best for her safety."

"What is best for her safety is for us all to work together to rescue her," Floyd said hotly. "Getting yourself killed won't save her."

"I have to meet the Destroyer's demands or she will die."

"Floyd is right," Adams said softly. "The Destroyer will not keep his end of the bargain to free Jane."

"That's my decision to make," Brandon said.

Adams considered for a moment and then nodded."Floyd, tell him what he needs to know."

"But—" Floyd spluttered.

"Tell him."

"No!" Floyd said. "Not until he sees reason!"

"Floyd—"

"He's not thinking rationally," Floyd protested. "He's—emotionally compromised, I believe the phrase is. He shouldn't be making decisions for anyone, let alone Jane."

"He seems to be rational to me," Adams said.

"You didn't see him last night," Floyd retorted.

Adams frowned. "You told me Speedy threw you into a wall."

"He did! And then Brandon tried to finish the job."

Brandon stood abruptly. "You are withholding information vital to the safety of the woman I love," he exclaimed. "I will do anything to protect her and if you insist on standing in my way then you are no better then those monsters—"

"I am trying to protect her," Floyd shouted at the same time. "The fact that you can't see that just shows how incompetent you are at attempting to save her. Until you get your emotions under control you need to—"

"—and while I don't want to fight with you, you leave me no choice. Because nothing, *nothing* is more important then saving Jane. Not my own life, and certainly not yours."

"—be locked away somewhere where you can't hurt yourself, or anyone else. I can take you in a fight, Brandon, and I swear, if you try to hit me again—"

Adams swore violently.

For a moment no one said anything.

"Is this true?" Adams asked thunderously, turning to Brandon.

Brandon's face went white, and the fight drained out of him. "Yes," he whispered. "It is."

"I'm sorry," Floyd mumbled, pressing a hand over his face. "I wasn't planning on bringing that up."

Adams fought to get himself back under control. "Floyd," he said quietly, "tell Brandon where the rendezvous is supposed to take place."

"But—"

"Just do it."

"Belmont View at midnight," Floyd said hollowly.

"You have your information," Adams said coolly. "If you wish it we will assist you in any way possible to save Jane's life. And then I never want to see your face again, is that clear?"

Brandon stood, magnificent in his height and costume. "I wish to extend my sincerest apologies for my behavior last night," he said. "As Mr. Floyd indicated, I was not thinking rationally and—"

"I don't care," Adams interrupted. "Do you want our assistance or not?"

Brandon was taken aback by the curtness of the reply. "The Destroyer demands my surrender," he said finally. "I dare not jeopardize Jane's life by refusing to comply."

He swept majestically out of the room.

There was a long silence in which nothing at all was said, and a great deal understood.

"He's going to get himself killed," Floyd said at last, still mumbling. "He's going to get himself killed, and Jane is going to die too. The Destroyer doesn't do things halfway."

"So go save the day," Adams said.

Floyd stared at him like a deer ready to bolt.

"Go," Adams said. "Take whatever—and whoever—you need. Be the hero for once."

Floyd pulled himself together, ideas beginning to spin in his mind. "I think," he said slowly, "I think I can do that."

A GOOD DAY
TO DIE

Belmont View was an office complex in progress. The shell of the building was two-thirds completed, and metal scaffolding framed it in a bizarre pattern of lattice-work. A crane loomed over a stack of steel girders ready to be lifted into place for the next floor. Welding equipment and other tools were locked into a steel crate nearby. The area in front of the building was clear, and lit by floodlights; waiting.

Brandon reached the rendezvous five minutes before midnight. He forced himself to remain calm, squeezing his hands into fists at his side to keep them from trembling. He stepped into the lighted circle and glanced around.

"Hello?"

An evil laugh emanated from the shadows. He whirled towards it, but the voice that called his name came from behind him.

"Blue Shadow!" the Destroyer boomed. He stepped out from behind a stack of steel girders holding Jane in front of him like a shield. One hand held a knife pressed up close to her throat. She had her eyes closed and her face was as pale as death.

"Jane," Brandon breathed, taking a step towards her.

"Nuh-uh-uh," the Destroyer warned, pressing on the knife. Jane made a little gasp of pain. Brandon froze, torn between anger and anguish.

"Let her go," Brandon said, trying to muster some defiance. "I'm here. You have what you want. Now let her go."

"I don't think so," the Destroyer said with a stony smile. "I think you should apologize first."

"Apologize?"

"On your knees," the Destroyer said.

"I don't think so," Brandon spat. "The deal was—"

"There was no deal," the Destroyer cut him off. "You do what I say, and I won't kill her. Now...on your knees."

Brandon hesitated. The Destroyer moved the knife from Jane's throat to her cheek and made a long shallow cut from her ear to just under her chin. Jane stiffened against him and suppressed a cry of pain.

"No!" Brandon said, panicking. "Don't hurt her! I'll—I'll do it. Whatever you ask."

He knelt awkwardly in the gravel yard. "I apologize."

"Hmm, nice try," the Destroyer said. "But a little sparse, don't you think? Try this: I apologize for humiliating you, great master."

Brandon bristled. "You are not my master!"

The Destroyer moved the knife over half an inch.

"I apologize for humiliating you," Brandon said hurriedly. "Great master," he added through gritted teeth.

"Again."

"I apologize for humiliating you great master."

"I don't think I quite heard that."

"I apologize—"

"Oh what have we got here?" Floyd jumped over the chain link fence and landed with the grace of a cat. "I'm not interrupting, am I?"

"What are you doing here?" Brandon hissed, his temper rising.

"Saving your life," Floyd tossed off.

"I told you—"

"I don't take orders, especially not from caped crusaders idiotic enough to call a mountain of stone like this "great master.""

Beneath his mask Brandon flushed in shame.

Floyd turned his attention to the supervillain.

"Not another step," the Destroyer warned, pressing the knife back to Jane's throat.

"Or what?" Floyd taunted. "She dies? You really think that threat is going to work on me?"

"Her blood will be on your hands," the Destroyer said uncertainly.

"You know that taking hostages doesn't work with me," Floyd tossed off. "Kill her or don't kill her but get her out of the way so we can get on with things."

"Don't—" Brandon begged, coming to his feet.

The Destroyer smiled. "Blue Shadow," he said, "My loyal servant. Dispense with this annoying bit of garbage for me."

"With pleasure," Brandon snarled. He yanked on Floyd's collar, pulling him around to face him, and punched him in the face before shoving him with as much force as he could muster into a pile of cinder blocks.

"Stay down," the Destroyer ordered, as Floyd started to stand up. A cry of pain from Jane reinforced the order. Floyd didn't move.

"I thought so," the villain said, smiling villainously. "You really do care about her."

Floyd didn't answer; didn't move.

With his free hand the villain tossed Brandon a second knife.

"Cut off his fingers," he ordered. "One at a time. I want to see if they grow back."

Brandon couldn't disguise the tremble in his hand as he picked up the knife and approached Floyd.

"I'm so sorry," he whispered.

Floyd showed no more emotion then mild surprise. "You're really going to let him do this to you?" he asked.

"He's going to hurt Jane," Brandon hissed.

"He's going to hurt her anyway," Floyd pointed out. "He's going to kill her, eventually. And then he'll kill you. And then you'll both be dead. Together."

"What are you getting at?" Brandon demanded letting his anger overshadow his shame.

"He is going to take your love and your life," Floyd said with certainty. "You're going to let him take your honor as well?"

Brandon glanced at Jane, her face pale and drawn with the faint trace of tears mingling with the blood on her cheek. "I don't have a choice."

"You always have a choice."

"Not this time."

Floyd's hand closed over Brandon's wrist and twisted sharply. Brandon let the knife drop with a cry of pain.

"I'm sorry," Floyd said, picking it up. "If anyone could have made me believe in heroes it would have been you, Brandon. But you're not one."

He threw the knife.

The Destroyer stumbled back with a cry of pain as it buried itself in his left eye. He let go of Jane, who fell. Brandon rushed forward and caught her. The Destroyer pulled out the knife and tossed it aside in disgust.

"You think I can be killed that easily?" he roared. "You puny, defiant—"

His iron-like fist swung down towards his two hostages in a crushing blow. Floyd got there first.

"Get her out of here," he ordered Brandon. "Just go."

Brandon gathered Jane in his arms and started towards the gate. Floyd dodged the Destroyer's large, swinging fists and darted behind the pile of cinder blocks.

"You don't know my weakness," the Destroyer roared at him. "We both know how this fight is going to end!"

"You don't know what I don't know," Floyd taunted. "Or what I do know, for that matter."

The villain picked up a few cinder blocks and started throwing them. Floyd ducked and they smashed into the locked equipment crate.

"You might not want to do that," Floyd suggested. "You could blow something up."

"You're worried about that?" the villain sneered. He threw another block at Floyd and as the defender dodged the Destroyer caught him, and threw him after the blocks into the crate.

Floyd landed in a tangle of cables and cords and generators and propane tanks. When he tried to stand his left leg screamed in agony, probably broken again. He snarled in pain and collapsed back into the chaos, deciding to lay still for a moment and take inventory. There were cutters and hammers and tool belts and drills and welding equipment. Surely in the midst of all this potential weaponry there was something that could kill the Destroyer.

He had a thick, impenetrable outer shell—how impenetrable, Floyd didn't know. He hadn't had time to research properly, and now he was going to have to improvise. Assuming he couldn't be stabbed, shot, or killed in any of the usual ways, Floyd was going to have to try a unique tactic—something that would kill him from the inside. Poison then. Or suffocation. Or—

"Destroyer!" Brandon yelled. Floyd swore under his breath and scrabbled at the chaos, yanking his weapon of choice out of the chaos.

The Destroyer's evil laugh resonated across the open space. "So, the little hero returns," he taunted.

"You and I have some unfinished business," Brandon said, standing bravely in the open. "Come and face me!"

Floyd closed his eyes and forced himself not to enter the verbal fray.

The Destroyer laughed. "Oh yes, the brave little mortal soldier, marching to the rescue. You could have left him here, you know. There was no need to come back."

"Yes, there was," Brandon retorted. "I forgot something."

"And what was so important it was worth risking your life to retrieve?"

"My honor."

Floyd swore under his breath and tried to stand again, but it was no use. For his plan to work he was going to have to force the villain to come to him. Whether he knew it or not, Brandon was necessary to make his plan work. Then again, Brandon was only mortal and he was facing down a walking statue with his bare hands. The hero didn't stand a chance.

The Destroyer stepped into the combat. Brandon dodged his first blow, but the second one knocked him halfway across the yard. He came back to his feet almost instantly, dusty but undaunted. He and the villain danced around each other like professional boxers, testing defenses and weaknesses. The blows Brandon landed on the Destroyer hurt him more then the villain. Floyd knew from experience that punching that hard outer shell was about as useful as punching a brick wall. Brandon was fighting fair, giving his opponent too much ground. In a fair fight he would never win. Then again, he probably wouldn't win in an unfair fight either.

Floyd cupped both hands around his mouth and yelled. "Brandon!"

The hero glanced at him, weary and distracted, and Floyd waved the acetylene torch in one hand and gestured with the other. Brandon's eyes widened—whether in understanding or pain Floyd didn't know as the Destroyer took advantage of his moment of distraction to drive an iron fist into the hero's stomach and send him flying into a pile of steel girders. Brandon got to his feet slowly, backing cautiously away from the Destroyer and towards Floyd. Floyd gripped one side of the steel cage and stood up, careful to keep the weight off of his bad leg. He made sure he had a firm grip on the welding rig and waited for his opportunity.

And on one level, he had to admit that Brandon was really good. Ten minutes into the fight and he was still standing—more than Floyd could say for himself. He moved warily now, aware of the Destroyer's ability to incapacitate him. He didn't know how to exploit the villain's weakness so he fought much in the way Floyd had—dodging and staying out of reach, hoping to throw his opponent off balance. And while he did, he led the Destroyer step-by-step to where Floyd waited.

Brandon was dangerously close to giving away Floyd's location when he feinted, drawing the villain's attention, then ducked and rolled between his legs. The Destroyer roared in anger, turning as quickly as he could manage to see where Brandon had gone.

Floyd was mere inches behind him when he shouted his name. The villain turned to him in surprise. He turned the knob on the welding torch he'd brought with him and blue flame sprang into life.

"What do you think that will do?" the villain taunted. "Flame cannot hurt me. I am impervious to—"

Floyd silenced him by jamming the torch into his open mouth. The flame bypassed his thick outer shell and began to burn from the inside out. The villain tried to scream but his voice was swallowed by the heat. The smell of burning flesh began to fill the air.

In the open yard Brandon watched in horror, and Floyd avoided looking at him. The villain was incapable of making a sound, but his agony was unmistakable. Floyd pressed on grimly, forcing him back against the cage and holding him there as his face slowly melted inward.

"Enough," Brandon said finally, coming towards him. "It's done, Floyd. He's dead."

He took the torch away gently, turning off the flame and tossing it away. The body of the villain soon followed, crashing to the ground.

"You're alive," Floyd said softly.

"Yeah," Brandon said. "Where you hoping otherwise?"

"You're alive," Floyd repeated. "I'm alive. Jane—"

"Jane is fine. I left her in safe place before coming back to finish the fight."

"You came back," Floyd parroted. "You could have taken her and gone. You *should* have—"

Brandon smiled. "Don't tell me what I should have done. You couldn't have won without me."

Floyd's eyes widened and he glanced again from the body of the villain to Brandon. And then he began to laugh.

❮ ❮ ❮

He was still laughing half an hour later when Adams and Finnley arrived.

"What happened?" Adams asked, approaching warily.

"We won," Brandon explained. They sat with their backs to the wreckage. Jane was asleep in Brandon's arms. "The villain is dead."

"So what's wrong with him?" Adams asked, nudging Floyd's leg.

He stopped laughing abruptly, hissing in pain. "I broke it again," he explained, in response to Adams' look.

"That's why the doctors tell you to stay off of it," the policeman pointed out.

"I know," Floyd said, and started laughing again. "I know."

The ever-stoic policeman lost his patience. "What do you find so funny?" he demanded.

"Look," Floyd said, gesturing broadly. "Count us. All three. We're alive. We all survived. Even I—"

He broke off helplessly. Adams glanced at Finnley. The constable merely shrugged.

"All right," Adams said, giving up. "Let's get everyone in the car and—"

"Wait a minute," Floyd said, holding up a hand to stop him. "Wait a minute. You're going into professional mode."

Adams folded his arms and waited.

"I know why," Floyd said. "So I should tell you, before we proceed, that Brandon did try to cut my fingers off during the fight."

"There was a supervillain involved," Brandon defended himself, nudging Floyd.

"There was a supervillain involved," Floyd agreed. "Also a woman."

"A very beautiful woman."

"A woman of substantial beauty and considerable grace and kindness."

"Is this going anywhere?" Adams asked, raising his eyebrows once more.

"Yes, it is," Floyd assured him. "I just forgot where."

"Mutual trust and cooperation," Brandon prompted.

"What he said," Floyd said. "It's over. It's in the past. Clearly he has impulse control issues where beautiful women and supervillains are involved, but there are worse people in the world."

"I don't follow," Adams said.

"I hereby give Brandon permission to beat me up any time Jane is kidnapped," Floyd said. "I just want to make sure you're okay with that."

"I'm not okay with that," Adams said. "I'm not okay with that at all. And I don't understand—"

"And it will never happen again," Brandon interrupted. "It just took a little violence to work out our differences. But now I realize that Floyd is very capable at what he does, and his methods do not make him dishonorable."

"And I realize that wearing a stupid costume doesn't imply stupidity," Floyd said.

"Okay," Adams said slowly. "So what you're trying to say is—"

"I'm only talking because if I stop I'll pass out," Floyd said. "So figure it out already."

"All right then," Adams said. "Shut up so I can take your friend to the hospital."

Floyd was still smiling when he fell asleep.

EPILOGUE

When Brandon and Jane walked into Adams' office, Floyd looked up at them from his desk in the corner and started laughing again.

"Are you ever going to get over that?" Brandon asked, trying—and failing—to put a note of disapproval into his voice.

"No," Floyd said with a chuckle. "Never. You're my good luck charm, Brandon. The inexplicable happens when you're around."

Jane gave her husband's hand a squeeze. "Don't tease the man," she said. "He deserves to have something to laugh at."

"So," Adams said, interrupting Floyd's amusement. "You're leaving then?"

"London doesn't need me," Brandon said. "You're in capable hands."

Floyd stopped laughing abruptly. "You're still going to fight supervillains?" he asked.

"Yes," Brandon said. "That's my calling."

"You're insane."

"I know that."

"You're certifiably—what did you say?"

"I know that," Brandon said, smiling at his expense. "You proved your point very well, thank you."

"And you haven't decided to quit?" Floyd's eyes were troubled. "When I got the wedding announcement I assumed—"

"That I'd chosen love over duty?" Brandon asked, raising an eyebrow. "You think I could ever make that kind of choice?"

"You did," Floyd said. "You have. Whether you accept it or not. The Destroyer is one supervillain out of thousands. How long do you think it will be before someone else gets the same idea and this time you *don't* win the battle?"

"I'm willing to take that risk," Jane interjected. "I wouldn't have it any other way, in fact."

"Wait," Floyd said, rubbing his eyes. "You were captured, tortured, and almost killed."

"Yes."

"Explain to me again—why are you willing to let that happen?"

"Death is inevitable," Jane said. "It will come to us all at some point. And to die without having loved is the true tragedy of the universe. I am not afraid to die if that is the price of being with the one I love."

"But intentionally going after supervillains—"

"Is who my husband is," Jane interrupted. "It is his identity—and it is why I love him."

"But—"

"It is worth it," Jane repeated. "I know you don't approve, Floyd, and I pity you for that. Your life is a cold, and lonely place whether you are aware of it or not. Honor never dies. Courage never dies. We are but fleeting parts of a great cosmos and to sacrifice the greatest gift we have been given in hopes of living just a few years longer is folly."

Floyd lowered his eyes, unable to meet her gaze.

"I hope you find someone," she said, cupping his face with her hand. "Someone for whom you are willing to sacrifice everything—even the world you're so desperate to protect. You may dismiss love as an irrational weakness but without it..." she smiled sadly and let her hand drop. "Without it everything you do is meaningless."

Floyd stood and turned away, gazing out the window. Behind him he heard Adams asking polite questions, exchanging pleasantries, and eventually bidding the newlyweds farewell and safe voyage. Brandon interrupted his reverie, touching his shoulder, and holding out his hand.

"Happy hunting," he offered.

Floyd shook his head. "I wish I could say the same," he answered. "Keep her safe."

"I will," Brandon promised.

And then they were gone, off to find a new life across the sea. There was a moment of silence before the policeman came to stand next to him, staring at the grey skies and the city below.

"Are you okay?" Joseph finally asked.

"Not even remotely," Floyd confessed.

Adams waited.

"I broke up with Kate."

Eyebrows raised. "I didn't realize you were together."

"Well—I kind of told her I never wanted to hear from her again."

"Ah."

Floyd turned to observe him. "You don't sound surprised."

"I talk to my sister," Adams explained. "She'd sort of let me know something was going on along those lines."

Floyd didn't answer, looking back out the window.

"You did the right thing," Joseph said after a long moment.

"Really?" Floyd asked, not realizing until too late how much bitterness he put into the word. "Then how come I can't make myself believe that?"

"Floyd—"

"I'm not supposed to care. It wasn't even supposed to be a possibility because this isn't my world. I'm not human. And even if I were—I'm not normal. I shouldn't even be capable of love. I don't even know what it is."

"Floyd—"

"All I know is fighting and hatred and manipulation..."

"I would die for you," Joseph said, silencing him with the admission.

A clock on the wall ticked away the seconds. A fly buzzed against the glass pane, trying to get out. Floyd clenched his hands into fists, trying to get his breathing under control.

"Why," he said in a near whisper, not trusting himself to speak more loudly. "Why would you say something like that?"

"To prove a point," Adams said, calm as ever. "Love isn't as complicated or as simple as you think it should be. It's not something you can just write off as non-existent or non-applicable. And it's not something you can escape from. Not on this world."

"I wish—" Floyd whispered, and left the words hanging between them like a broken thread.

"Sometimes the right decision isn't the best one," Adams offered. "She asks about you. She forgives you."

Floyd didn't answer.

"If you like, then the next time she calls I can tell her you said hi."

"No," Floyd whispered.

"Are you sure?"

"Yes." He straightened up, his confidence returning. "I'm not so arrogant that I'll risk someone else's life for my happiness."

The adventure continues!
Keep up with new releases, updates,
contests, supervillains and more at
<u>supervillainoftheday.com</u>.

Keep reading for a sneak preview of the next
exciting adventure—coming soon!

The yellowed phone which was the only piece of equipment adorning the otherwise empty office space buzzed. Floyd picked it up and said: "Department of Supervillains. No humans allowed."

"This is DI Casey," said a woman's brisk voice on the other end. "I take it from the insolent greeting that you are the infamous Mr. Floyd."

"I didn't realize my infamy had spread that far," Floyd said with a grin, "But otherwise yes, this is he. What can I do for you?"

"My department has been receiving a number of prank calls," Casey said, her voice marred by impatience. "We're not allowed to dismiss them out of hand but I don't have the man power to spare to actually look into them. This is a courtesy call to let you know that I'm having the file delivered to your department and I expect a report by lunchtime tomorrow."

Floyd took the phone away from his ear and stared at it, as if the device could somehow explain the conversation.

"Mr. Floyd?" Casey repeated. "Do you understand me?"

"Um," Floyd said. "I think I need to let you talk to my superior officer."

"A simple 'yes ma'am' will suffice," the detective said.

Floyd glanced helplessly around the empty room. There was no one to help him.

"Yes ma'am."

Casey hung up on him. Floyd replaced the phone in its cradle and stared at it. Finnley walked by with an armful of folders and paused to smile. "Desk duty, Floyd?"

Floyd shook his head, trying to clear it. "What department does DI Casey work with?"

Finnley's grin widened.

"What?" Floyd demanded. "What's the joke?"

The elevator dinged and a petite young woman in a blouse and skirt stepped out. She looked exhausted and a bit harried, brushing stray pieces of blond hair out of her eyes.

"Hello," she said, looking around at the empty desks. "I'm looking for Mr. Floyd with the DSV?"

"That's me," Floyd said. "Can I help you?"

"My name's Essie," she said, holding out a hand. "Essie Carmichael. DI Casey sent me down."

"You don't look police," Floyd observed.

"I'm not," Essie said. "I'm Casey's personal secretary. She pays me out of her salary. The position came recommended and I haven't had a better offer but it's—"

"Trying?" Floyd guessed.

She smiled. "I'm supposed to brief you on this case and reiterate that she wants a report by tomorrow noon."

"I don't know who DI Casey is," Floyd said, choosing his words carefully, "But I'm not an investigator to look into prank calls, neither am I a clerk to be writing reports. Casey was lucky to catch me at all. Come noon tomorrow she won't be able to find me to find out where her report is."

"I know," Essie said, her voice more of a sigh. "I know. I don't expect you to run around doing her bidding, but she does. I wish I could offer you some advice but—"

The phone rang. Floyd reached for it but Essie was closer and answered it reflexively.

"Department of Supervillains. How may I help you?"

She paused, listening. "Of course. Just a moment."

She handed the phone to Floyd. "It's Inspector Adams for you."

"Hey Joseph," Floyd said.

"You found a secretary?" Adams said. "Already? You? You hate secretaries."

"She's just visiting, actually," Floyd said.

"Do you like her?"

"Yes."

"The odds of that happening again are second to none," Adams said. "Put her back on."

Floyd handed the phone out to Essie. "He wants to talk to you."

"Hello?" Essie said, and spent the next several minutes listening, occasionally saying things like "yes sir" and "I think so" and just once "But I don't think DI Casey—"

When she hung up the phone her cheeks had turned slightly pink. "I'm being transferred to your department," she said, glancing at Floyd. "Immediately."

"Congratulations," Floyd said. "Now tell me what I need to know."

"Well..."

When she smiled she had a dimple. "I'm twenty-three years old, and I have two sisters— one older and one younger. I speak French and play piano but my real skills are organization and negotiation. I'm also brilliant at stalling a waiting client; indefinitely. Oh, and I have photographic memory."

She paused for breath.

"That's great," Floyd said. "But I was asking about the prank calls."

"Oh dear," Essie said, blushing again. "I tend to talk too much when I'm nervous. Or excited. I'm sorry."

"Which one is it?" Floyd asked. "Nervous or excited?"

"A little bit of both," she stammered. "I'm sorry. This is just all so sudden. Oh dear, what am I going to tell Casey? She's expecting me back by now. She's going to be so furious!" Her eyes widened in fear and her hands began to shake.

"Hey, hey, hey," Floyd said, reaching out to reassure her. "Don't panic. I'll take care of it."

"You will?"

"I'm not infamous for nothing," Floyd said. "Don't worry about it. It will be fine, I promise. Adams wouldn't have said your transfer was immediate if he couldn't back it up."

"O-okay," Essie said. "If you're sure."

"I am," Floyd said. "Now tell me about these prank calls."

"Okay," Essie said, pulling herself together. "There were three of them. All within ten minutes of each other, all from the same general area."

"What area?"

"Woodhaven. You're familiar with it?"

Floyd grunted an affirmative.

"One was a teenage boy. One was the mother of a twelve-year-old girl, insisting her daughter had seen something. One a history professor at Cambridge. Their stories were different, but their claims were the same. They'd all seen something."

"Seen what?"

"A dragon, Mr. Floyd. A fire-breathing dragon."

Don't miss the start to an exciting new
supervillain series!

Visit shraid.net for more information.

ABOUT THE AUTHOR

Katie Lynn Daniels has been writing since she was eight. She quickly made the jump from short stories to novels, but was never able to muster the word count needed to qualify as "epic." She finally settled down with the form she's best at—novellas.

She also writes children's picture books, a wide variety of poetry, and a blog of opinions. In addition she is a singer/songwriter, indie filmmaker, Kentucky dairymaid, and big sister in a family of nine.

Follow her on her blog: katielynndaniels.com
Or stalk her on twitter: @authorkatielyn